Home Farm Twins

Scott

The Braveheart

Jenny Oldfield

Illustrated by Kate Aldous

Hodder
Children's
Books

a division of Hodder Headline plc

Special thanks to year 7 pupils of Ludlow Church of England School, and to the children of Richmond Church of England Primary School.

First published in Great Britain in 1999
by Hodder Children's Books

10 9 8 7 6 5 4 3 2 1

A Catalogue record for this book is available from the British Library

ISBN 0 340 72795 0

Typeset by Avon Dataset Ltd, Bidford-on-Avon, Warks

Printed and bound in Great Britain by
The Guernsey Press Co. Ltd, Channel Isles

Hodder Children's Books
a division of Hodder Headline plc
338 Euston Road
London NW1 3BH

One

'Whoa!' David Moore cried. He pulled on the reins.

His big chestnut thoroughbred carried on trotting round the indoor arena.

'Whoa!' he shouted, panicking. This was his first ever riding lesson, and it was proving harder to stop a horse than he'd thought.

Helen and Hannah giggled. Their dad bounced in the saddle.

'He's ... completely useless!' Hannah whispered.

'Yep.' Helen leaned on the fence and grinned.

She steadied the camera and peered through the viewfinder.

'He's not using his legs.' Hannah watched him jiggle up and down. His hard hat had tilted forward over his eyes, his voice had risen to a squeak.

'Nope.' Helen got ready to take the shot, then yelled an order: 'More legs, Dad! You need to grip with your calf . . .'

'Who-ooo-a . . . ah!' The twins' father finally lost his balance and fell to the sawdust floor.

'. . . muscles!' Helen and Hannah chorused. 'Use your calf muscles!' Too late. Their dad had bitten the dust.

Click-click-click! Helen took the action shots. The horse went on trotting round the circle without his rider.

'Never mind, Mr Moore!' Jeanie Watson ran to help him up. A trim figure in black jodphurs and a cream Aran sweater, the riding instructor hauled him to his feet and brushed him down.

'Sorry about that.' David Moore looked round sheepishly as he took off his helmet. There was sawdust all over his baggy jumper and in his ruffled, wavy hair.

'Not at all. Full marks for effort!' Jeanie consoled. 'Considering that was your first time in the saddle, you didn't do so badly.'

'First and last.' Mr Moore rubbed his sore elbows and shook his head. Then, while Jeanie went to catch the runaway horse, he limped across to Hannah and Helen. 'How come I let you talk me into this on the last day of our holiday?'

The twins grinned back at him, their brown eyes twinkling from underneath their thick, dark fringes.

'It's easy, Dad!' Hannah insisted.

'Nothing to it,' Helen agreed. Carefully she slid the camera back into its case and tapped it gently. 'And it's all here on film,' she told him. 'David Moore's first riding lesson. Location shots at Invermore Riding-School, Invermore village, Loch Shiel, Scotland!'

Helen, Hannah and David Moore had spent a week of the summer holidays with the Saunders family, renting Benmore Cottage, two miles up the coast from Invermore. They'd left behind the twins' mother, Mary, who'd had to stay in Doveton to run her cafe. Though they'd missed her, their dog, Speckle, and their farmyard full of animals, they'd had a brilliant time.

'Day One,' Hannah read from her holiday diary as they sat on the grass waiting for their dad to pay Jeanie Watson for his lesson. 'Went to the beach. Swam in the sea. Sea was freezing. Had fish and chips for supper.'

'Saw seals in Loch Shiel,' Helen reminded her. 'Go on, add that bit!' Three seals had bobbed up to them as they swam to a rock in Benmore Bay. Their sleek grey heads had looked like shiny rubber, their dark eyes had been huge.

Hannah added an extra sentence. Then she flicked the page and read on. 'Day Two. Went to the beach. Swam. Laura's mum made egg sandwiches for lunch. Chicken and chips for supper at The Highland Lassie.'

'You've written loads about food,' Helen pointed out. 'But nothing on the animals we've seen. What about the Shetland ponies on the beach?' She remembered following the hoofprints across the sandy bay, turning a corner into a rocky inlet and seeing the sturdy little ponies trekking out from the riding-stables there.

Hannah tilted her head and looked sideways at her twin sister. She turned to the back of the book and pointed. 'Special section on animals. "Day Two. Shetland ponies. One chestnut, two black, three pintos. Shaggy manes, short legs. Would love to take one home to Home Farm." Satisfied?'

Helen nodded. 'Here comes one now!'

A small, chubby girl of about six had just ridden a white Shetland pony into the paddock where they sat. The pony picked up his feet and pricked his ears, glad to be out in the sunny field. Smart in black jacket and velvet hat, white trousers and black boots, the girl rider trotted the pony towards some jumps.

'See, Dad!' Hannah heard David Moore come up behind them. She watched the pony clear one jump, then another, his short legs pounding over the ground, his thick mane falling low over his

sweet face. The little girl turned him and rode at some higher jumps.

'Easy-peasy!' Helen murmured as the pony cleared these too.

'Hmm!' Their dad cleared his throat. 'I could do that, no problem.'

The girl thundered her pony close by at full gallop, racing at still higher jumps. The pony took off and flew through the air, landed safely and galloped on.

'Er-hum!' Helen was busy unzipping her dad's

fancy new camera which he'd brought to Scotland to work on a special project for a horse and pony magazine. She pressed a button which said 'Print'. Soon the camera produced a picture which she held up for him to see.

Hannah snapped her diary closed, jumped up and peered over Helen's shoulder. The picture clearly showed David Moore falling off his horse and landing on the sawdust floor.

'Just need a bit of practice . . .!' he muttered red-faced, as the twins stood and laughed.

'A digital camera, eh?' Geoffrey Saunders examined David Moore's new piece of equipment. 'No film needed? Contains its own printer. Very, very clever.'

'I get instant results,' David Moore explained, 'so it's useful for the work I do.' He spread examples of his pictures round the kitchen table at Benmore Cottage, swiftly taking out the one of him hitting the deck. The rest were shots of Shetland ponies on the beach, or ponies backed by rolling hills rising to the steep peaks of nearby

Benn Thurnish and Benn Eyre. Chestnut ponies with long fringes and big brown eyes, black ponies with barrel-shaped bodies and stumpy legs. And dun, piebald and skewbald ponies raising their heads and gazing thoughtfully at the camera as David Moore had clicked happily away.

Hannah, Helen and Laura Saunders sat around the table with the grown-ups.

'It's our last afternoon,' Laura sighed, staring dreamily out of the tiny square window, down a grassy slope to the beach where they'd spent most of their holiday. 'What shall we do?'

'Climb a mountain!' Helen suggested brightly.

Hannah groaned.

'Swim in the sea!' Helen was already on her feet, running for her swimming-costume.

'Too c-c-cold!' Hannah objected.

Helen dashed back down the stairs. 'Go and look at the ponies!'

'Yeah!' Hannah and Laura sprang up together. They raced for the back door.

'Don't pester Jeanie!' Laura's mother, Valerie Saunders, warned as the three girls disappeared out of the gate. 'Remember, she has a riding-school to run!'

'Well, I'll be sorry to see you girls go,' Jeanie Watson told them.

Laura, Hannah and Helen had spent the afternoon helping to muck out stables and groom the horses.

'Not half as sorry as we will be to leave,' Hannah told her. She put the curry combs and brushes back in their boxes.

'Except that when we get home we'll see Speckle and Solo.' Helen reminded her about their dog and pony waiting for them at Home Farm. 'And Mum, of course.'

She stood back to admire the last of the beautifully groomed ponies they had turned out into the field at the back of the riding-school. She was a tiny brown mare, under ten hands high, with a wide face and small ears almost hidden by her thick thatch of black mane and forelock. The moment she trotted into the field, she gave them a knowing glance, sank to her knees and rolled over into a patch of fresh mud.

'Oh, thanks very much, Dolly!' Laura sighed.

The twins giggled as Dolly rolled again, kicking her little legs in the air in sheer delight.

'Dolly's the latest addition to the school,' Jeanie explained. 'She's five years old and a bit of a handful, as you can see.'

'She's lovely!' Hannah sprang to the muddy pony's defence.

'Ah, but I'm hoping she'll calm down a wee bit when we get another new one to keep her company.' Jeanie's face relaxed into a smile at Dolly's games. The pony was up on her feet and curling her top lip at them, as if giving them a cheeky grin. 'I'm on the look-out for a good Shetland right now, as a matter of fact.'

Helen listened quietly to the stable owner's plans. She gazed out over the field to the hills covered in pale purple heather, dotted with tiny white farmhouses, and beyond that to the hazy peak of Benn Thurnish.

'Shetlands are sturdy little creatures,' Jeanie Watson told them, letting the breeze blow her sandy-coloured, wavy hair back from her freckled face. 'They're used to hard work, and they're good with children. And what's more, they don't mind the harsh winters we get up here.'

Hannah nodded. She agreed with everything the riding-school owner had said.

'They can be shy . . .' Jeanie went on, breaking off as, at that very moment, Dolly came trotting over and poked her nose straight into Laura's jacket pocket.

'Yeah!' the girls chorused.

'. . . *sometimes*. They're *always* alert and quick to learn.'

Dolly found a mint tucked into the corner of the pocket. She grabbed it expertly between her lips and drew it out.

'Right!' Laura cried.

'And they have such spirit. They never give in,' Jeanie said, singing the praises of the miniature breed.

'Brilliant!' Helen agreed as Dolly trotted off with her stolen sweet.

'Perfect,' Hannah murmured. Almost small

enough to squeeze into the back of their car and drive home to the Lake District . . . if only!

'Such brave little horses,' Jeanie concluded.

They all gazed at muddy, cheeky, adorable Dolly.

'Come on,' Laura sighed and glanced at her watch as she dragged the twins away from their favourite holiday activity. 'Time for us to go.'

Two

'Oh-ah-oh!' David Moore creaked downstairs early the next morning.

'What's up, Dad? Are you stiff?' Helen asked sweetly. She'd packed her bag, had breakfast and was ready to leave.

'All over! Every single bone in my body aches.'

Hannah was on the phone, talking to their mum. 'Dad can hardly move,' she told her. 'He went riding yesterday and fell off.'

Mary Moore laughed. 'Tell him, at his age he should have more sense!'

'She says you should have more sense,' Hannah reported. The corners of her mouth turned up as she watched him creep across the kitchen to pour himself a cup of tea.

'Huh. Tell her, Thanks for the sympathy.'

'So, listen, what's been the best bit of your holiday – besides seeing your dad fall off his horse?' Mary asked.

Hannah thought hard. 'The mountains,' she began. 'And the lochs. Going swimming, rowing boats. The food – we've had chicken and chips three times. Oh, and riding the ponies!'

'Sounds just like home.' Her mum chatted on, 'Solo's missed you. I can see him through the window right now. He's up at the wall, sticking his head into the farmyard, saying, Where have those two girls got to?'

'Tell him we're on our way.' Hannah pictured their grey pony and the rides they would soon have up Doveton Fell.

'Make sure you've packed everything and don't leave anything behind. And say thank you to the Saunders for inviting you. And tell Dad to drive carefully.' Mary Moore issued a list of last-minute instructions.

Hannah promised, then said she would have to go. 'Helen and Dad are loading the car,' she told her mum. 'We're setting off before Laura and her mum and dad because our car doesn't go as fast. And because he wants to be back in time to do some work.'

'OK, see you this afternoon.'

'Yes, bye!' In the end it was a hurried farewell, as her dad called her to bring her bag to the car.

'Sandwiches for the journey!' Valerie Saunders followed Hannah out and thrust a lunch-box through the car window.

'Helen, you forgot your trainers!' Laura dashed out and tipped the shoes into Helen's lap.

'Here's the map. I've marked a route.' Geoffrey Saunders, calm as ever, strolled towards the driver's side of the loaded-down car. There were bags in the boot and strapped on to the roof rack, and a jumble of bats, balls, snorkels and flippers were stuffed into the pockets on the back of the front seats. 'You head for Benn Thurnish, and a steep, difficult pass through the mountains called Glendach. After that, it should be plain sailing. It's a more direct route than the way you came.'

'Thanks.' David Moore took the map, then fastened his seat belt. He turned the ignition and the engine croaked slowly into life.

'Bye!' The Saunders stood and waved from the yard of the rented croft as the Moores set off for home.

'Bye!' they chorused back.

'Home in six hours,' David Moore predicted, pointing the car at the distant mountains and settling down for the journey.

'Famous last words!' Helen groaned.

They were sitting on a grassy bank by the side of the road. Whenever they looked, the steep grey rocky slopes of Benn Thurnish towered over them. On the road in front of them, their ancient car wheezed and panted.

'Find a phone-box and call the AA, Dad,' Hannah suggested quietly.

The car bonnet was up, steam was hissing out

of the engine. David Moore stood nearby, his sleeves rolled up, his hands and arms covered in black grease.

'Just give me another sec,' he insisted. 'I'm sure I can fix this.'

Helen raised her eyebrows and sighed. 'Like he fixes bookshelves and door-locks at home!' she whispered.

'Shh!' Hannah watched him dive into the depths of the car's engine once more. She went to fetch the box of sandwiches that Mrs Saunders had packed for them, offered one to Helen and began to munch.

The winding route up Benn Thurnish and along Glendach Pass had been too much for their poor car. It had chugged its way out of Invermore, past Jeanie Watson's stables, and away from the rocky coast. It had wound its way inland, across the heathery hills, past small, stone crofts into high country where the farmhouses were deserted, the land wild and lonely.

'That's funny,' their dad had said, as the car engine whined and lost power.

'Dad, what's that steam coming up from under the bonnet?' Helen had asked, halfway up the old cattle pass of Glendach.

He'd stopped the car at once, muttering the words, 'fan belt . . . radiator . . . cooling system.' And here they were; marooned, with only a box of sandwiches to keep them going, and no chance of getting home in the planned six hours after all.

Hannah polished off her sandwich and looked round. The pass followed a narrow gap through the mountains, twisting and turning, sometimes cutting through cliffs. There were signs all the way along warning cars how steep the hills were, or telling you to beware of falling rocks. When the car had broken down, almost at the very top, their dad had only just managed to freewheel it off the narrow road on to a patch of scrubby, short grass and gravel.

'No wonder no one lives here,' Helen said to Hannah, frowning up at the overhanging cliffs.

'Spooky,' Hannah agreed.

'No one ever drives up here except us!' Looking down the empty road, then up at the cloudy sky,

Helen spotted a hawk soaring and hovering over some poor, unsuspecting prey – a mouse, perhaps, or a baby rabbit. She decided to stand up and scare the bird away.

Hannah watched her. 'Where are you off to?'

'I'm gonna make sure that hawk doesn't get his lunch.' Helen looked for a way up the rock on to a heather-covered slope beyond. Then, finding footholds, she went ahead, with Hannah following close behind.

'Don't go far!' David Moore glanced up from his struggles with hoses and clips.

'We won't!' the twins sang out.

Hannah clambered up the rock, noticing the bird flap his wings and wheel away across the moor. But they went on climbing anyway, deciding that exploring the pass was far more exciting than watching their dad repair the car.

After five minutes careful climbing, and with a bird's-eye view of the winding road below, Helen was the first to reach the heathery slope. She caught her breath and checked that the hawk had flown well away.

Hannah joined her. The wind whipped through her hair and gave her goose-pimples on her bare arms. She shivered and walked on up the slope, feeling the scratchy heather tug at her feet and trip her as she went. 'There's an old farm up here,' she told Helen, pointing to a run-down, single-story building a few hundred metres to their left.

'It looks like no one's lived here for years.' Helen took in the broken windows, the holes in the roof. 'But look, there's still a path leading to it.'

Helen and Hannah could just make out a pale track through the dark heather. It ended at two stone gateposts without a gate. A low wall surrounding the croft was overgrown with blackberry bushes. The farmyard was dotted with yellow dandelions, and, as they drew nearer, they saw that grass grew up through the cracks in the front doorstep.

As Helen went ahead to test the door, Hannah stopped and looked round. Had she imagined it, or had she heard a noise from round the side of the old building? She listened carefully. Yes, there it was again. A breathy noise, followed by footsteps, perhaps. Hannah froze and warned Helen. 'Listen!'

Helen spun round on the overgrown doorstep. 'What?'

'I'm not sure. There's something or someone round that corner!'

'There can't be!' Helen protested. 'We're miles from anywhere. The place is a wreck!'

'I know, but listen!' Hannah heard it again. Loud, deep breaths, then feet striking a hard surface. 'I think it's an animal. Something big!'

At this, Helen's frown eased and her eyes lit up. 'A deer!' she suggested. This was good deer country. 'It could be a stag with great big antlers!'

The idea made them dash for the side of the house before the creature took fright and ran away. Together they rounded the corner.

'Oh no!' What they saw took Hannah by surprise.

Not a deer, but a pony. A black and white Shetland tethered on a short rope to a stake of wood. He stood on a patch of open ground where the grass had been cropped to bare earth. His

black mane was matted, his coat dull. And the cruel rope stopped him from reaching the lush grass that grew only a metre or so from where he was tethered.

'He's starving!' Helen cried.

Hannah gasped. 'Poor thing!'

He was looking at them, backing away, pulling at the rope until the ragged headcollar he wore dug into his cheek.

'Who did this?' Helen stared at the pony in disbelief. He was about ten hands high, with a black face and a white star on his forehead. His shoulders and forelegs were black, with white socks. But the white patches over his whole body were mud-stained, his tail a straggly mess of bramble sticks and burrs.

Hannah held Helen back. 'Don't go near. He's scared of us!'

The Shetland pony pulled at the rope until the collar cut his cheek. He flattened his ears and stamped at the ground.

'No, I don't think he's frightened.' Helen watched closely. The pony wrenched his head to the side, his eyes rolled, he stamped and snorted. 'It looks more like he's warning us off.'

'From what?' Hannah looked to left and right. The pony seemed to be guarding a spot by a clump of heather behind him. And now that she studied the heather more closely, she saw a movement there too.

Helen spotted it at the same moment. There was another black and white shape in the purple heather, but smaller than the tethered pony, about the size of a large dog. It was struggling to its feet on thin, gangly legs, its heavy head hanging. It shook as it stood, wobbled, then suddenly let its legs collapse under it. It was down again, only its head showing, making a high whinnying sound as if calling to the tethered pony for help.

'It's a foal!' Hannah cried. She ran forward and dropped to her knees beside the struggling creature.

The other pony strained at his rope, tried to rear and strike out. There was blood on his face from a cut that was deep and dirty.

'Watch out!' Helen warned.

The pony's hooves thudded down close to where Hannah crouched over the foal.

'She can't stand. She's too weak!' Hannah was almost in tears to see the starving, frightened baby. She ignored the flailing hooves and cradled the foal's head in both hands.

'Who did this?' Helen demanded again, staring round the overgrown farmyard and down the deserted slope towards Glendach Pass.

Her voice drifted over the heather, into the glen and was swallowed by the bleak hills opposite.

'. . . Who did this?'

There was no answer. Only silence, and the sound of the wind whistling through the heather, the high-pitched cry of a bird soaring overhead.

Three

'Such brave little horses!' Jeanie Watson's recent words echoed in Helen and Hannah's heads as they watched the piebald Shetland pony defend the motherless foal. 'They have such spirit. They never give in.'

The defiant pony tugged and kicked. He pulled so hard that the wooden stake that had been hammered upright into the hard earth to hold him prisoner began to lean sideways.

'Whoa!' Helen approached cautiously to try and steady him. Though he was small, the pony was strong. If he landed a kick, she knew how much it would hurt.

Meanwhile, Hannah worked out what was wrong with the foal, who trembled, but lay quietly in the heather beside her. 'I don't think there's anything wrong with her legs,' she decided. 'She's just really thin and weak. With no mother to look after her, I guess she hasn't been able to feed properly.'

'This one's doing a pretty good job of looking after her,' Helen pointed out. The bold little pony was still warning them off and tugging at his rope.

'Let's call him Scott,' Hannah decided. She didn't like the sound of 'this one' or 'the piebald pony'. She felt he deserved a name. And since they'd found him in the heart of the Scottish Highlands, she thought that the name Scott suited him.

'And this one can be Heather, because that's where we found her.' Helen crouched down beside Hannah to study the foal. 'Scott and Heather.'

'I wonder where her mother is.' Hannah stroked her head and soothed her.

'And how long have they been here?' Helen gazed all around, hardly able to believe that the ponies had been abandoned without food or water.

As Helen grew angry and her expression darkened, Hannah tried to think ahead. 'What are we going to do?'

Helen frowned and stood up. 'We're going to rescue them,' she said sharply. 'What do you think?'

'OK, OK. Don't bite my head off. What I mean is, how?' It was one thing saying they would rescue the ponies, another thing deciding how to do it. After all, the foal was too weak to stand, and the little stallion too angry to let them near. 'We need help,' she told Helen firmly.

Helen thought, then nodded. 'You stay here. I'll go and tell Dad.'

She was gone almost before the words were out of her mouth; round the side of the deserted croft, across the heather and disappearing down the cliff towards the road.

Hannah sat on in the breeze. Bees hummed and

buzzed amongst the purple flowers, the sun felt hot on her shoulders and back.

Could these be wild ponies? she wondered. Maybe no one owned them, and they'd been born to wander free over the Highland glens. Then some mean horse thief had come along and captured them. It was part of a plan to take them away and sell them. Only the plan had gone wrong, and for some reason the sneaky thief had been forced to tie Scott up and leave him here. But why leave Heather as well? And why not tie her up too?

As Hannah waited, she made up a story to explain why the ponies had been abandoned. She looked again, this time with even more concern, at Scott. If only he would stop struggling and accept that she was here to help. But no; he pulled and rubbed at the sore place on his face, wrenching at the rope by turning his head and straining against it with his strong neck. The wooden stake leaned at an angle but held fast.

He reared up on to his hind legs as before, tugging the stake in the opposite direction, making it sway and loosen in the earth. Hannah winced and looked up, saw his hooves paw the air. No, he wasn't a wild pony; his feet were neatly shod with iron shoes. It meant he had an owner after all; someone who had mistreated him and left him to starve.

Scott landed with a thud and pulled once more at his tether. The whites of his eyes showed as he turned and twisted, struggling to get free. He seemed to be edging nearer to Hannah and Heather, urging the foal to her feet. She had raised her head from Hannah's lap and had bent her thin legs under her, trying to take her weight and lift her frail body.

And now Scott was straining at the rope with all his might, inching the stake out of the ground until at last it gave way. The spirited pony had pulled it clear. He was free.

'Hurry, Helen!' Hannah yelled across the stretch of moor. She crouched forward as the pony realised that the tether had broken and made a charge straight at her. She heard his hooves thud, felt the ground shake as he approached. Then, at the last moment, she dived sideways, away from the foal, and rolled clear of the charging horse. Scott surged between her and Heather, dragging the rope and stake along the ground. Quickly, he swerved and turned and came back towards the foal.

Hannah rolled, then got to her feet, breathless with surprise. She saw the pony push with his head, nosing Heather up off the ground.

Then Helen reappeared. She saw that Scott had broken free and began to run across the moor. 'Dad's on his way!' she shouted to Hannah.

Scott had managed to get Heather on to her feet. He raised his head and trotted a few paces, warning Hannah off with a fierce squeal. Then he waited for the foal to follow.

Heather tottered; one, two, three steps forward. Then her knees buckled. Down she went, deep into the bushes, her hooves tangled in the woody branches. Then up again, struggling back on to her feet, trying to escape while Scott stood guard.

'Don't!' Hannah protested. She could see that the foal was too weak, that no way could she follow Scott up the steep mountain slope.

But the determined pony wouldn't give in. Once more he approached the foal to urge her on. It would have been easy for him to give up on Heather. He could have broken free and saved himself from the strangers who seemed to threaten him. By now he could have been galloping up Benn Thurnish, trailing the rope, with no chance of being caught.

Instead he stayed. He nudged softly at the foal's trembling body as a third figure approached the deserted croft.

'Dad, what are we going to do?' Helen pleaded. She watched with tears in her eyes as Scott stuck by Heather, even though he risked his own freedom.

David Moore swiftly took in the situation. 'Stand back,' he warned Helen and Hannah. 'I'll see if I can recapture the pony. But watch out for his hooves. When I grab the rope, he isn't going to like it one little bit!'

'He's a fighter, you must admit.' The twins' father stood back after he'd finished hammering the stake back into the ground. He dropped the heavy stone he'd been using and heaved a sigh of relief.

The black and white pony had bucked and kicked, twisted and turned to escape. But David Moore had held fast to the rope long enough to knock the spike of wood firmly into the ground, and now Scott had to admit defeat. He stood, breathless and sweating, nostrils flared and ears laid back.

'If only he could realise we're trying to help,' Helen murmured, one wary eye on Scott, the other on the weak foal who lay collapsed in the heather.

'I feel so sorry for him,' Hannah breathed.

'What now?' Helen turned to her.

'I think we should get Heather under shelter somehow.' She glanced around the open hillside. Although the day had started sunny, there were big black clouds gathering over the high peaks of Benn Thurnish and Benn Eyre.

'Good idea,' their dad agreed.

'Then we should find something for her to eat.' Hannah thought that the small foal's main problem was hunger. 'By the look of her, I'd say she was about six months old . . .'

'Which means she was born in early spring,' Helen broke in, nodding in agreement. Heather was almost as tall as the fully grown Scott, but she was gangly and skinny, and seemed to be only half the size around the girth and across her shoulders. Her black mane and tail were still the short, soft bristles of a very young horse.

'. . . so she probably doesn't need her mother's milk any more, but she does need loads of protein and special vitamins and stuff in her feed. By the look of things, she's just been dumped and left to get on eating the grass round here as best she can.'

'There's not much grass that's fit to eat on these scrubby slopes,' David Moore pointed out. 'And no water for her to drink, as far as I can see.'

'Let's try taking her into the old farmyard,' Helen suggested quickly. They had to move fast. 'Maybe we can find a tap that still gives running water.'

Hannah agreed. 'I think I saw some kind of barn by the house. We could carry Heather and put her in there. It'll be out of the wind, and if it rains, she'll stay dry at least.'

'Dad, will you carry her?' Helen asked. 'Hannah and I will hold Scott back in case he tries his escaping trick again.'

So David Moore went quietly forward, ignoring Scott's angry stamps and snorts. He eased his arms under the foal's body, keeping her long legs tucked in. Heather raised her head and struggled feebly.

'Hurry up!' Helen pleaded. Both she and Hannah had seized Scott's rope and were leaning with all their weight to stop him from following their dad and the foal.

David stood up with Heather in his arms. He stepped carefully through the gorse and heather towards the croft, then on to the overgrown track and through the gateway. Looking across the weed-covered yard, he saw that Hannah was right; there *was* a low barn with a wide wooden door that swung open on creaky hinges. He headed straight for it and stepped inside.

'I think Scott's calmed down a bit,' Hannah whispered. The pony had stopped pulling at the rope and instead watched anxiously. 'Will you be OK with him if I go in after Dad?'

Helen nodded. 'Don't be too long!'

So Hannah went ahead. Inside, the barn was dark but dry. Cobwebs brushed against her face and bare arms as she fumbled forwards. Then her eyes got used to the dim light and she made out low beams overhead, a wooden loft, stone walls, old feeding stalls for cattle, a piece of rusting iron machinery. 'How is it?' she asked her dad.

'Fine!' he replied. 'The roof probably leaks in places, but we can find a dry spot. There's even some old bales of straw in the loft. We can use it for bedding!'

'Ugh!' Hannah exclaimed as her cheeks came into contact with more cobwebs. Wiping her face, she quickly nipped up a ladder into the loft and began shifting a straw bale towards the edge.

'I'm still worried about the car,' David said, choosing a dry corner for Heather. 'I should try and stop someone to ask for help. But dare we leave Scott and ask Helen to come in here to help you?'

Hannah sighed as she tipped the bale on to the

floor. Then she climbed down the ladder, pulled the bale to pieces and spread the straw to make a bed. At last, David was able to crouch down and lay the foal there. 'I'll ask her,' she decided. 'And I'll look for a water tap while I'm out there.'

She sped off once more. Out in the yard she spotted an old plastic bucket. That would do to carry water into the barn. Now for the tap.

She looked round again.

'Hannah?' Helen called from round the corner of the derelict building. She must have heard busy footsteps.

'Yep, hang on a sec.' Hannah had spotted a tap and ran to try it. To her relief, clean water gushed out. She called again over the noise from the top.

'Helen, Dad wants to know if we can risk leaving Scott while you come into the barn and he goes back to the road, to see if he can flag someone down!'

'Tell him that's OK!' As soon as the bucket was half full, she turned off the tap. She would take this to the foal, then come out for more water and take it to Scott.

So Hannah rushed back into the barn, slopping water as she went. 'This should do it!' she gasped, out of breath from the effort. She put the bucket down by the newly-made straw bed, giving her dad Helen's answer as she went down on her knees by Heather's side. Then, as David dashed off for help, she waited for Helen to join her, stroking the foal's neck and speaking softly. 'Here's some nice, fresh water,' Hannah told her. 'Drink it; it'll make you feel better.'

Heather didn't respond. She lay motionless in the straw, her eyes half-closed, her frail body shaking.

Frowning, Helen crouched by the foal's other side. She reached out a hand to stroke her, then was afraid to touch. 'She's going to be OK, isn't she?' she asked Hannah.

Hannah looked across at her with troubled eyes. 'I don't know,' she said softly. 'I only wish I did!'

Four

'The bad news at this end is, we need a new hose for the radiator,' Hannah and Helen's dad reported, leaning out of the driver's window with a worried face.

The twins had raced across the moor and scrambled down the cliff to the roadside to tell him how poorly Heather was.

'In the end we did manage to get her to drink some water,' Hannah had gasped.

'Now she's asleep in the straw,' Helen had added. 'But she needs food. Dad, we've got

41

to get her something to eat!'

He'd nodded and passed on the grim news about the car. 'We can't move from the spot until we have a new hose.'

'What are we going to do?' Hannah groaned. 'Poor Heather could die of starvation while we're sitting here waiting for help!'

But Helen was busy scanning the Glendach road, following its winding course back into the valley the way they'd just come. 'Do you want to know the *good* news?' she said quietly and pointed to a speck in the distance.

'What?' Hannah cried, spinning round to look.

David Moore got out of the car.

'The Saunders are coming up the hill.'

Hannah and David followed the direction of Helen's pointing finger. And there, crawling towards them like a shiny silver beetle was their friends' car.

It climbed and climbed in the silent glen, growing bigger, then disappearing behind a rocky outcrop, appearing again along a straight stretch of road.

Helen and Hannah stood impatiently. The car was still a long way off, but now they could hear the whine of its engine as it began to climb the steepest part of the hill.

'Mr Saunders will be able to fetch us a new hose for the car!' Hannah ran a few steps down the road to meet them.

'And feed for Heather!' Helen added.

'We hope!' David Moore warned. 'But don't count on it.'

The twins ignored him and ran on. They waved with both hands and yelled out the moment they saw the car crest the hill.

Mrs Saunders wound down her window, leaned out and called to them. 'Hannah, Helen, whatever are you doing here?'

In the back seat, Laura too leaned out of her window.

'Car . . .'

'. . . broke down!'

'Hill . . .'

'. . . too steep!' Hannah began and Helen finished each garbled sentence.

'Shetland . . .'

'. . . pony . . .'

'. . . and a foal . . .' Hannah's throat was dry from running and calling out. She stopped by the side of the road as the Saunders' car drew level. 'We found them up there by that old croft, just dumped!'

'The foal's sick!' Helen explained to Laura, while Geoffrey Saunders stopped the car, got out and strode on up the hill to join David Moore.

Then, while the two men discussed the problem with the car, Valerie Saunders listened carefully to the twins' account. She studied the map laid across her knees, obviously wondering what they should do now.

'How far to the next town?' Laura's father came back to join them, followed by David Moore.

'Over twenty five miles, on mountain roads – it's beyond Benn Thurnish,' Mrs Saunders reported.

Hannah looked at Helen and shook her head. At this rate, they'd never get help to Heather in time.

'I vote we turn round and go back to Invermore,' Valerie suggested. 'For a start, we know the town, and there's a garage there that should be able to help with the spare part for your car.'

Laura nodded eagerly. 'And Jeanie Watson at the riding-stables will have hay for the foal!'

'OK.' Her dad agreed and got back into the car. 'It should take us a couple of hours there and back.'

Once more, Helen and Hannah exchanged worried glances.

'Hang on!' It was Laura's turn to make a quick decision. She whispered to her mum and they both seemed to agree. 'I'm staying!' she announced, her long, fair ponytail swinging as she hurriedly got out of the car. 'I want to see if there's anything I can do for this Shetland pony and the sick foal!'

'That's great, Laura!' Hannah gasped as the three girls climbed the hill. She led the way to the broken-down croft. 'We told Dad you'd be able to help!'

David Moore was still down at the roadside,

giving details about the punctured hose to Valerie and Geoffrey Saunders.

'And you know everything about horses!' Helen added, relieved that their older friend was with them this time. Laura had looked after her own pony at Doveton Manor since she was small and had been Solo's owner before the twins had him.

'Not everything,' she said quietly. But she looked determined as they approached the farm building.

Hannah led her through the gateway and their hurried footsteps pounded across the stone flagged yard. Hearing them from round the side, Scott gave a loud, angry whinny that made Laura stop in her tracks.

'Maybe I should take a look at him first,' she suggested. Without waiting for Helen and Hannah's reply, she changed course and ran towards the sound.

Scott stood tethered where David Moore had left him. Angry and frustrated, he trotted in a tight, frenzied circle, straining at the rope, demanding to be freed. There was a patch of dark sweat across his shoulders, his eyes rolled as he tugged and the worn halter dug deeper into his sore cheek.

Laura frowned at the sight and shook her head.

'We can't leave him, can we?' Hannah murmured. Every second was cruel and she felt ashamed at not having helped him sooner.

'But if we let him go, he could run off,' Helen pointed out.

'Unless . . .' A new idea formed in Hannah's mind. 'There are those cattle stalls in the old barn,' she reminded Helen. 'Maybe we can get Scott inside one of those!'

'I think that's a good idea. It means he'd be close to the foal for a start,' Laura agreed. 'That is, if we can persuade him to co-operate.' Cautiously Laura approached the pony. She walked steadily up to him without showing any fear, letting him know with soothing words and gestures that she didn't mean him any harm.

Scott saw her and fixed his gaze on her. His ears stayed back, but his trot slowed. He listened to her words.

'Easy, boy!' Laura murmured, as Helen and Hannah stood well back. 'Let's get you away from here.' Reaching out to untie the rope from the stake, she kept on talking and reassuring.

'She's doing it!' Hannah whispered. Scott wasn't shying away, or kicking and bucking. He'd gone quiet and still.

'No one wants to hurt you,' Laura told him gently. She inched closer, running her hand up the rope until she could stand in against his shoulder and begin to lead him. She turned him towards the croft, clicked her tongue and gave him a command. 'Walk on, boy!'

'She's brilliant!' Helen sighed, watching Laura lead Scott quietly on.

The twins followed, then overtook Scott and Laura in the farmyard, showing them the way into the barn.

'Easy, boy!' Laura talked smoothly and led him on. 'The thing is, ponies can sense things,' she told Hannah, who stood holding the barn door open. 'They know if you're going to be mean to them. And the opposite; they can tell if you're trying to help.'

'Bring him this way,' The darkness of the barn

made Helen lower her voice to a whisper as she showed Laura and Scott to an empty stall.

Overhead, a swallow darted from a roof beam, dipped and flew out through the door. In one corner, a rustle of straw told them that Heather was now awake and stirring.

Scott too heard the foal's movements. He turned his head and snickered.

'Yes, you're right,' Laura told him in a low voice. 'Hannah and Helen have taken care of the foal. Everything's going to be fine.'

The pony's ears were up, flicking this way and that. His eyes took in every nook and cranny of the strange, derelict barn.

'And now we're going to take care of you,' Laura told him. 'We're going to put you in this nice, safe stall, and we're going to bring you feed and water.'

Obediently brave little Scott followed where Laura led.

'You're a good boy,' she told him, turning him round in the narrow stall so that he stood facing out towards Heather's corner. 'What we need is something to tie across the entrance so he can't wander out,' she explained to Helen.

Helen looked round for a length of rope or a bar of wood that might slot across the opening to the stall.

'Here!' Hannah found some pieces of old fencing propped against a wall.

Together she and Helen made a barrier to keep Scott in. Then they stood back with a sigh of relief.

'He's a working horse, if you ask me,' Laura told them, studying the tiny pony's sturdy limbs, his strong neck and straight back. 'He's probably been used to pull a cart. I don't think he's been kept as a pet.'

Helen listened. 'He's great, isn't he?'

Scott's ears flicked in her direction. He watched warily for further signs of life from the far corner.

'He's beautiful!' Laura agreed. Then she went quietly across the barn to where Heather lay. 'And so is this little one.'

'Do you think Scott's her father?' Hannah asked, dropping to her knees beside the heap of straw, telling Laura how he'd given up his own freedom to look after the foal. Heather raised her head and whinnied softly.

'He could be.' Laura shrugged. 'Their markings are similar, but I couldn't really say.' Then she ran a hand over the foal's flanks and sighed. 'She's really, really thin.'

Helen and Hannah caught the worry in her voice.

'We have to wait for your mum and dad to get back with the feed,' Hannah whispered.

'Then what?' Helen asked.

'Then we make sure Heather gets plenty to eat,' Hannah said, softly stroking the foal.

'I know that. But, I mean, then what?' Helen wandered away to the door and looked out across the deserted yard. 'Who do these ponies belong to? What's going to happen to them next?'

From his new stall, Scott threw back his head and whinnied.

Laura looked up. There were frown lines between her eyebrows, her jaw was set in a determined line. 'Then we hire a trailer and take them both back to Doveton!' she announced in a strong, clear voice. 'We've got plenty of room in the stables at Doveton Manor. I don't care what anybody says, Scott and Heather are coming home with me!'

Five

'First things first,' Valerie Saunders insisted.

Hannah, Helen and Laura crowded round the straw bed to watch Heather pick at the handful of feed which Laura's mother held out for her. They held their breaths and kept all their fingers crossed as slowly the foal began to munch.

'Let's try and get this little lady back on her feet.' Mrs Saunders brushed aside Laura's big plan and concentrated on her task. 'Jeanie Watson gave us a mix with special supplements; high energy, high protein. She says there should be enough in this bag to last three or four days and whoever looks after the foal should give the feed little and often.'

'What about hay?' David Moore asked. He stood behind the girls, arms crossed, looking on with concern as the weak foal ate a second handful of grain.

'We can give her that too; same principle of little and often,' Geoffrey Saunders replied. Then he turned to Laura and spoke seriously. 'I want you to think through this idea of yours about bringing the ponies to the manor.'

Hannah and Helen crossed their fingers more tightly than before. Tall and severe-looking, Mr Saunders was someone you didn't argue with. They stole glances at Laura's frowning face, then looked across at Scott.

'For a start,' he went on, 'you need proof that they've been abandoned. If these two horses *have* an owner, he or she is not going to be too pleased when they comes back and find them gone without so much as a by-your-leave!'

'Yes, but if Helen and Hannah hadn't come along and rescued them, poor little Heather wouldn't have survived!' Laura reminded him. The tension amongst the group gathered in the old barn rose. 'She'd have starved to death. And Scott would have broken free eventually and run off. *Then* where would the so-called owner have been?'

'Even so.' Valerie Saunders finished feeding the foal and stood up. 'We still wouldn't be within our rights to take the ponies. I agree with your father, Laura; until we can be sure that Scott and Heather were left here for good, we simply can't make a decision about their future.'

'I knew it!' Helen mumbled to Hannah, uncrossing her fingers with a sigh. Laura's idea had been too good to be true. She went over to Scott's stall and put her arm round his neck.

Hannah followed. 'Mr Saunders gave us this tube of ointment for the cut on Scott's cheek,' she told Helen in a subdued voice. 'Jeanie told him it's a good antiseptic cream, and we should clean the wound, then put it on.'

Helen nodded and took off the pony's headcollar. She found a clean handkerchief in her pocket, which she dipped into Scott's water bucket and then dabbed at the cut. He stood patiently, keeping his head still even when the cream went on.

Hannah winced. 'That must sting.'

'You're a brave boy,' Helen told him. But she couldn't help sighing as she considered what Laura's parents had said.

'Are you giving in?' Hannah heard the defeated sigh and challenged it. 'As easily as that?'

'No!' Helen retorted, her cheeks flushed. She stroked Scott's soft muzzle as he thrust his nose against her hand. 'Who said I was?'

'It just sounded like it.' Hannah's mind flew on. 'So, we have to prove they've been dumped. Fine. Let's do it!'

'How?' Helen lowered her voice even further as she saw Laura end the argument with her mum and dad by turning on her heel and dashing from the barn.

Hannah faltered. 'We ask around,' she said vaguely.

Leaving Scott with a final pat and stroke, Helen and Hannah followed Laura. 'Who?' Helen asked as they came out of the barn into the bright daylight. She scanned the empty miles of hills and mountains. 'Who do we ask?'

Suddenly something caught Hannah's eye. She screwed up her face and squinted into the sun. She pointed high up the slope to a clump of trees and a small white house. The remote farm was the nearest sign of life. 'Them!' she decided. 'Unless you've got a better idea.'

She didn't wait for Helen or Laura to argue, but set off at a run for the far-off cottage.

'Not so fast!' a voice yelled from a Land Rover before Hannah, Helen and Laura had covered even half the distance from the deserted croft to the tiny farm.

A grey and white dog leaped from the back and streaked down the hill towards them. Then a man climbed down from the driver's seat and followed.

'Uh-oh!' Laura stopped in her tracks, grabbing hold of Hannah and swinging her round to look at the angry man. Helen, too, waited until the dog reached them, keeping a wary eye on its snapping jaws.

'Good boy, Bobby!' The man's gravelly voice praised the dog as he approached. Dressed in a checked cream and brown shirt and working trousers, he glowered at the three girls. 'You're on private land, where you've no business to be.'

'We're sorry!' Helen was the first to catch her breath. 'We didn't realise!'

'Aye well, you do now.' The crofter stood his ground, keeping his dog crouched and alert at his

side. He was a short but sturdy figure with dark hair and a weatherbeaten face.

'We wanted to ask a question,' Hannah broke in. She ignored the growls from the dog and took a step forward.

'About the old croft?' He nodded briefly down the hill to the deserted farm. 'I know nothing about it. It's been run down like that for years.'

'No, not about the farm,' She rushed on. 'About the two Shetland ponies . . .'

He shook his head impatiently. 'I know nothing about them either.'

'Did you see them?' Helen asked. 'One was tethered round the far side of the farm. The other's just a foal . . .'

'We think they were abandoned!' Hannah cried. 'We're trying to find out who did it!'

'I didn't see anybody. I know nothing,' the man repeated, frowning suspiciously.

'Who else could we ask?' Laura looked in dismay around the empty hillside. The heather stretched on for ever, without another house in sight.

'Don't ask me. It's none of my business.' Calling

his dog, the crofter refused to offer help. 'All I'm saying is, this is my land and I want you off it!'

It was his final word as he turned and strode back to the Land Rover, the dog at his heel.

'If everyone's as unhelpful as that farmer, we'll never find out anything about the ponies!' Laura had dragged a reluctant Helen and Hannah back to the roadside. They found their fathers bent over the broken car engine, with Mrs Saunders hovering anxiously nearby.

'Shh!' she warned. 'It's like a surgical operation to get this new hose in place, but I think the patient is about to recover!'

'Pass me that last clip, would you?' David Moore stretched out an oily hand for the metal ring that Geoffrey Saunders held. He put it round the hose and screwed it into position. Then, after a few more moments, he emerged from under the bonnet, saw the girls and smiled.

'Is it fixed?' Hannah asked.

Her dad nodded.

'Does that mean we can set off?' Helen cried.

'Yes. Don't look so down. It's good news.' He wiped his hands on a rag while Geoffrey Saunders collected up the spanners and screwdrivers.

'But if we leave, what happens to Scott and Heather?' Laura wanted to know.

Valerie Saunders nodded. 'I know, I've been wondering about that too . . .'

'Yes?' Helen, Hannah and Laura urged. Maybe, just maybe Mrs Saunders was going to change her mind!

'. . . and I think the best thing to do is to ring the RSPCA,' she said quietly.

Helen felt her heart thud with disappointment. Hannah closed her eyes and turned away.

'Now, Laura, listen to your mother,' Mr Saunders jumped in ahead of his daughter's objections. 'The RSPCA are the very people who are equipped to deal with this sort of situation. If these ponies have an owner who can be traced, their inspectors can take them to court for unnecessary cruelty. And until then, the ponies will be very well cared for, believe me.'

David Moore looked on quietly, studying the

faces of each of the three girls in turn. But he said nothing.

'We can drive on and ring the nearest RSPCA office from the next town,' Mrs Saunders said kindly. 'You mustn't worry. I'm absolutely sure that Scott and Heather will be fine!'

And so, slowly, with a hollow, empty feeling, Laura, Hannah and Helen accepted the decision.

'Wouldn't you like to say goodbye?' Valerie Saunders asked as they hung their heads and got into the cars.

Hannah glanced at Helen, who shook her head. 'No, thanks.'

'Laura?'

'No . . . thanks.' It would be too much to bear, to see the little black and white ponies again, knowing that it would be the last time.

'Ready?' David Moore asked the twins as he got into the car. He glanced in the rear-view mirror at their glum faces.

Hannah and Helen stared blankly out of the window without answering.

'You did all you could,' their dad told them,

turning the ignition and starting the car.

'No, we didn't!' Hannah murmured. 'They could've had a good home at Doveton Manor!'

'But unfortunately it hasn't worked out that way.' David paused and glanced up the hill. 'It's a pity.'

Silence from the back seat. Hannah and Helen were too choked-up to reply.

'Wait a minute!' Quickly taking his camera from the glove compartment, their dad got out of the car. 'I'm just running up there to take a couple of photographs of the ponies,' he told the Saunders. 'It'll help the RSPCA to have pictures as proof of the mistreatment. I won't be long!'

The twins watched him disappear up the hill. While he was gone, Laura got out of her car and wandered across. No one had the heart to talk as they imagined David Moore going into the old barn to take the pictures.

But though Helen wasn't saying much, her brain was working overtime. She knitted her brows.

Hannah noticed the look of concentration. 'Helen's hatching a plan!' she warned Laura.

Helen ignored her. Then, when their dad came back, wanting to show them the successful shots, she began.

'They'll look great in the horse and pony magazine,' she told him, holding the photographs up for everyone to see. 'And they've got a good story behind them. You know, Cruel Owner Abandons Shetland Ponies Without Food Or Shelter!'

'Hmm.' Her dad looked over her shoulder and nodded. 'That's true. I could make Scott the main focus of my feature: Scott the Braveheart!'

'Great idea,' Helen encouraged. 'It's just a pity that, if we drive on now, we won't know the *end* of the story.'

Suddenly Hannah understood what Helen was up to. 'That's right!' she cried. 'You'll have great pictures and a really fantastic story . . . but without an ending!'

'Whereas, if we stay a couple of extra days to investigate what actually happens, you can carry on taking pictures and give the magazine a complete beginning, middle and end!' Helen said, leaning forward, her eyes eager and bright. 'The whole story!'

'Stay where?' their dad said. He was obviously listening to the plan, turning it over in his mind.

'A bed and breakfast place; anywhere!' Hannah seized on Helen's brilliant idea. 'Laura could stay too. We could all try to find out stuff for your magazine feature!'

'Scott's been so brave!' Helen sighed. 'He's a real hero!'

'And Heather's still poorly!' Hannah insisted. 'We don't even know if she's going to make it!'

'Hmm,' David Moore said again. 'I'd have to ring up and find out if it was OK with your mum.'

'Please, Dad!' Hannah and Helen urged. They could tell he was weakening.

'Please, Mr Moore,' Laura added quietly.

He frowned. He ummed and aahed. Then he got out of the car and paced up and down.

The girls followed his every move.

Then he came back and leaned in through the window. 'You win,' he told them. 'It's probably a mad idea, but let's give it a go!'

Six

'Glendach House: Bed and Breakfast'. Hannah read the wooden sign hanging by the gate of a tall, grey building on the lower slopes of the old cattle-pass. The house had ivy growing up the front and round turrets at each corner, like the towers in old fairy-tale picture books.

'I bet it's got a ghost!' Helen whispered. She watched from the roadside as their dad marched up the gravel path and knocked on the front door.

'And I bet the door creaks!' Laura warned, as it opened a fraction. 'Yes; listen!'

69

'Creepy!' Hannah breathed.

They'd found the house by taking a tiny side road over a stone bridge, having waved goodbye to Valerie and Geoffrey Saunders at last. Laura's parents had agreed to the new plan, leaving David Moore in charge of the girls and promising to inform the RSPCA about the plight of Scott and Heather in case he didn't get the chance. Then they'd wished them all luck and gone on their way.

Now it was well past midday and they were hoping that Glendach House would have empty rooms where they could stay.

'Yes?' A man opened the wide, arched door and stood on the top step. His voice was deep and gravelly, his face creased by a dark frown.

'Oh no!' Helen recognised him at once. She bobbed down behind the wall to hide. 'It's Mr Don't-Ask-Me!'

'The man from the moor!' Hannah remembered his voice and frown, sliding down beside Helen with a groan. 'The mean one who wouldn't help!'

Laura sighed and sank beside them. 'What's he doing here?'

'Come on, girls.' David Moore strode back to the gate. 'Our luck's in; Mr Firth says they've got two vacant rooms . . .' He slowed and peered round the corner. 'What are you doing down there?'

'Hiding!' Helen said in an obvious, over-the-top voice. She rolled her eyes and raised her eyebrows.

'I can see that. But what I mean is, why?'

The girls could hear the angry man's footsteps approaching down the gravel path. 'Because Mr Firth doesn't like us!' Hannah explained. 'We met him . . . earlier!'

She paused and froze, suddenly face to face with the grey and white dog who'd jumped out of the Land Rover and chased them. The sheepdog had dashed between David Moore's legs, turned the corner and discovered the crouching girls.

They stood up slowly, red-faced and nervous.

'Hmph!' The landlord of Glendach House saw them and made a grumpy snorting sound.

'Come along, bring your bags!' A second person came out of the house; a smiling, red-haired woman dressed in jeans and a white T-shirt. She stepped smoothly past the glowering Mr Firth, ready to help see her guests in. 'Bobby, move out of the way, there's a good boy.' She patted the dog as she passed 'Now, I've kept the rooms aired, ready and waiting for our next visitors. And it just so happens I've a fresh batch of scones just out of the oven . . . Oh, by the way, I'm Maggie Firth, and this is my husband, Angus.' The smile didn't falter as she bustled and ushered them in. 'Angus probably didn't introduce himself because he rarely does, but his bark is worse than his bite, believe me!'

Four scones and two cups of tea later, Hannah had got over her surprise and was ready to ask questions.

They sat in the Firths' oak-panelled living-room, looking out over the garden, across the glen to Benn Thurnish beyond. Mr Firth had gone out with Bobby to round up sheep, David Moore was taking a shower in his room, and Laura, Helen and Hannah were free to investigate.

'How come we saw Mr Firth up by the derelict

croft?' Hannah asked their good-natured landlady.

'Tut!' She tipped her head back as she collected plates and mugs. 'Don't tell me; let me guess. He told you you were on private land and ordered you off?'

Helen nodded, then polished off a fifth scone.

'Well, never mind. That's just his way. If it was up to me, I'd let visitors roam up there to their heart's content. After all, there's only the one wee deserted croft, and nobody to bother about trespassing on the moor.' Maggie Firth chatted on as before.

'Do you own the other farm, further up the hill?' Laura asked.

'Brae Croft? Aye, we do. We let it out as a holiday cottage. There's a man renting it now, as a matter of fact. A Mr McRae. He called by yesterday to see if it was free, and by chance it was.'

Helen steered Mrs Firth to the only subject that she, Hannah and Laura were interested in; Scott and Heather. She told their landlady about the mysterious ponies, then asked her advice. 'How could we find out more about them?'

'Go to Kindart,' came the prompt reply. The landlady's serious expression showed that she had taken the ponies' plight to heart.

'Where's that?'

'It's a wee village two miles down our lane, well off the beaten track. But it has a pub, a chapel and a shop, and all the folk from the farms round here call in at Kindart most days of the week.'

Thanking her, Hannah, Helen and Laura jumped up.

'Have you got the photos?' Helen reminded Hannah, who held up the pictures of Scott and Heather.

'Could you tell Mr Moore where we've gone when he comes down?' Laura remembered to leave a message as the twins rushed out down the long corridor to the front door of the ancient house.

'I'll say you're at Kindart,' Maggie Firth confirmed. 'And that you're investigating the case of the abandoned ponies!' she added with a sympathetic smile.

* * *

'No, I'm sorry.' The middle-aged woman behind the counter at The Country Kitchen shook her head. She handed the photographs of Scott and Heather back to Hannah. 'I know plenty of Shetland ponies belonging to the lassies round here, but I don't recognise those two.'

'Thanks anyway.' Helen stood in the doorway of the tiny general store, anxious to move on.

Laura hovered outside, glancing this way and that up and down Kindart's short main street.

'Try Jimmie McManus, the landlord at The Red Deer,' the woman suggested. 'If anyone knows where the poor wee things came from, Jimmie's your man!'

'This way!' Laura pointed to the pub a hundred metres down the road.

She ran ahead, towards the low building with a painted sign showing a magnificent deer with antlers.

Helen sprinted to keep up. 'She's going straight into a pub!' she gasped at Hannah, amazed at Laura's daring.

'Looks like it!' The door was open, the low sun

casting long shadows across the paved area in front.

But before their friend could dash inside, a broad, balding man with a double chin and a tea-towel slung carelessly across one shoulder appeared on the step.

'Whoa!' He blocked Laura's way with a good-natured cry. 'You must be the three lassies Maggie Firth told me about.'

Hannah and Helen slowed to a halt, bundling together behind Laura and looking up at bulky Jimmie McManus.

'News travels fast!' Helen murmured. Their landlady at Glendach House must have been on the phone to the pub landlord.

'I hear you've got some pictures to show me.' Mr McManus held out a broad hand and took the photographs from Hannah. 'Aye,' he said with a long sigh, 'they're grand ponies, these Shetlands. I kept one just like this for my wee girl. He was awful good with the bairns.'

'But have you seen *these* ponies before?' Helen broke in.

The landlord shook his head.

'Are you sure?' Laura insisted.

'I've not seen them, but I may have heard a wee whisper about them.'

'Oh.' Laura's face fell. She began to frown.

'There was a customer in here last night,' Jimmie McManus went on. 'A stranger. He happened to mention that he had a couple of Shetland ponies for sale.'

'Yes?' Hannah nodded and urged him on.

'That's it.' The landlord shrugged his broad shoulders. 'No one took him up on it, so he drank his beer and moved on.'

'But it was definitely two Shetlands?' Helen asked. 'Did he say what colour?'

Mr McManus took the towel from his shoulder and wiped the tops of the tables close to the pub door. 'Piebald,' he confirmed. 'Like the ones in your pictures.'

Laura's frown deepened.

'Did he say his name?' Helen asked.

'No.'

'And what did he look like?' Hannah had taken

the photos and slid them carefully into the back pocket of her jeans.

'Nothing special.' Jimmie McManus shook out the cloth and gave the girls a kind smile. 'An ordinary type; medium height, medium build . . . Oh, there was one thing I noticed!'

'What?' Helen and Hannah chorused.

'He did have a heavy bandage strapped around his right hand. The fingers were swollen and bruised. When I asked him how it had happened, he wouldn't say.'

'That's great, thanks!' Helen stored the vital piece of information.

'Let's go!' Laura muttered, as Hannah thanked the helpful landlord.

'Where to?' Helen wished she wasn't in such a hurry as she chased down the street after her.

'To see Scott and Heather,' she replied, her face pale and tense. 'I want to check that they're still there!'

'Do you feel better now?' Helen asked Laura from the safe, warm shelter of the ponies' barn.

The sun had sunk low behind the mountains, and the air had grown cool as the three girls made their hurried way from Kindart village back to the deserted croft.

Laura rubbed Scott's cheek. Then she parted his tangled forelock and stroked the white star on his forehead. 'No, not much better,' she confessed.

'How come?' Hannah had gone straight to Heather's corner of the barn to offer the foal water and food. The tiny pony looked rested and calm on her comfortable straw bed.

'I felt OK until Mr McManus told us about the man with the bandage,' Laura told them.

Scott nuzzled up to her, his small ears pricked, his lip curled so that he could nip gently at her T-shirt.

'Up till then I was convinced the ponies had been dumped,' she explained, resting one arm round Scott's neck. 'Which made things dead simple. No owner – no problem. We could adopt them and take them home to Doveton.'

'But . . ' Hannah let Heather take the oat mix from the palm of her hand. She felt the foal's tongue lick every scrap. 'If there's an owner after all, and he shows up to claim them, then we do have a problem!'

Laura nodded.

'Maybe the man in the pub won't come back,' Helen said. 'Look on the bright side; he tried to sell Scott and Heather, but he couldn't find a buyer. Maybe he got fed up feeding them, or couldn't afford it, or something. So he dumped them here and drove off. In that case, he's never coming back!'

'Helen could be right!' Hannah let Heather carry on licking her fingers. She looked across the dusty, dim barn at Laura and Scott.

Their worried friend nodded and gave a brief smile. 'Let's hope you're right,' she whispered. 'Because if that owner does come back, I don't know what we'll do!'

Seven

'Come on, girls, eat your breakfast!' David Moore said cheerfully.

It was early Monday morning and three tired faces stared across the table piled high with cereal, toast and fruit juice. No one had slept well in the narrow wooden beds in their spacious room overlooking Benn Thurnish.

'I've had enough, thanks.' Hannah pushed her plate away. Then she asked the question that had been on the tip of her tongue since dawn. 'Dad, would it be OK if we go and feed Heather now?'

Maggie Firth was clearing plates as she spoke. She sighed and shook her head at David Moore, as if acknowledging that he had his hands full trying to get Laura, Hannah and Helen to behave sensibly over the two Shetland ponies. 'Let me ask Angus to drive them over,' she suggested.

'No need, thanks!' Helen scraped her chair back from the table and darted for the door. A ride in the Land Rover with bad-tempered Mr Firth was the last thing they needed.

But at that moment, Maggie's husband opened the breakfast-room door. 'Someone at the door to see you,' he barked at his wife. 'Says he wants to pay the rent for Brae Croft.'

'That must be Mr McRae.' She put down the pots and went quickly out of the room. But she stopped and turned. 'Oh, Angus, these lassies would like a ride over to the old croft!' she called, before her footsteps echoed down the long corridor once more.

Hannah blushed. 'No, that's OK, thanks!'

'We'll walk!' Laura gabbled.

All three rushed to escape. But by the time

they'd pushed and shoved and tumbled through the door, Mrs Firth was standing at the front porch already deep in conversation with the visitor from Brae Croft.

The two figures blocked their way out of the house and their voices drifted down the narrow corridor.

'. . . It's been a short stay with us, Mr McRae,' Maggie said, pleasant as ever, as money changed hands. 'Two nights isn't nearly long enough to see the area properly.'

'I'm not on holiday, I'm here on business,' came the short reply. The thin, grey-haired man held out his hand for change. He stuffed the notes into the pocket of a shabby black padded jacket.

'And what kind of business might that be?' Maggie followed the stranger out over the threshold, letting Hannah, Helen and Laura edge out after her.

The girls ducked their heads shyly and made their way down the path.

'Did you see his hand?' Laura demanded, tugging at Helen's T-shirt.

'No. Why?' Helen glanced over her shoulder.

'He's wearing a bandage!' Laura's eyes were wide with disbelief and dismay.

'I'm in sales,' McRae replied vaguely to the landlady's question. He seemed anxious to pay his rent and be off, impatient at her relaxed, easy chatter.

'What do you sell?' she persisted.

Hannah gasped at Laura's news, then looked out into the narrow road. She saw a tall red van with a back that could be lowered to form a ramp down to the ground. The vehicle was designed for transporting animals of some kind.

'. . . Horses!' Helen gasped, guessing the answer. 'He sells horses!'

'I deal in Shetland ponies, if you must know,' McRae told Maggie Firth as the three girls stood open-mouthed. 'I've got four of them in the horse-box right now, though by rights I should have six!'

'Oh, really!' Maggie's voice went up with a sing-song note. She shot a meaningful look at the girls by the gate. 'What on earth happened to the other two?'

'Escaped,' McRae grumbled. 'Two piebalds. They ran off when I reached the top of the pass and parked by the roadside to give them their hay-nets. They must have broken loose from their tethers inside the van, so when I lowered the ramp, they shot straight out and up the hill.'

'And you couldn't catch them again?' Mrs Firth tutted and pretended to feel sorry for the horse dealer.

'He's the man!' Laura cried, beside herself with anger. 'He's Scott and Heather's owner!'

Hannah nodded and tried to calm her. As the landlady kept the dealer talking, it gave the girls time for everything to slot into place.

'Let's take a look in the van!' Helen hissed.

Quickly they crept out on to the road and tried to peer inside.

'Stand on the bumper and look through the little back window!' Hannah told Laura. 'Go on, you're taller than we are!'

So Laura climbed up and peered in. 'He was telling the truth; there are four ponies!' she hissed. 'They all look miserable. It's really dark, and I can't see any hay or water in there!'

'Right!' Helen said furiously. 'That's it!' she began to march back up the path towards the house.

'. . . The gelding's a vicious little beast,' McRae told Maggie, holding up his injured hand. 'He gave me a real fight when I finally managed to get the halter rope on him. He pulled and tugged so hard he cut my fingers to shreds!'

'Good!' Helen muttered to herself, still advancing up the path. The man deserved it for treating his ponies so badly.

'And by the time I'd got him safely tethered, the foal had vanished into thin air,' the horse dealer complained. 'A nice little weanling of five or six months. Would have made a perfect family pet.'

'Where did you tie up the gelding?' Maggie asked, apparently full of sympathy.

'Ah now, there's the thing!' The frown on McRae's shadowy, unshaven face deepened. 'I left him on a patch of grass near a deserted croft, thinking I could go looking for the foal and soon be on my way. But could I find the little nuisance?'

'Shh, Helen!' Hannah darted forward to warn her not to interrupt. 'Let him finish!'

'I looked up and down that hillside and there was no sign of her. So I decided to call it a day and leave her behind.'

Maggie's eyes widened. 'But was she old enough to suvive up there all alone, Mr McRae? The nights on Benn Thurnish can be awful cold, even in midsummer.'

He shrugged. 'I can't afford to be sentimental. I have a business to run.'

Helen, Hannah and Laura bit their tongues and pressed their lips together to stop themselves from crying out in protest as they pictured tiny little Heather alone and loose on the dark moorside.

'In any case, by that time on Saturday evening it was too late to drive on to the riding-school in England where I've already got a buyer for the whole bunch of them. And that was the reason I decided to stay on at Brae Croft. It gave me a chance to ask around that evening and next day to see if anyone was interested in buying the piebald, so I didn't have the bother of driving him another couple of hundred miles. But I had no luck there either. In the end, I've decided to forget about the missing foal and bundle the gelding back into the horse box. But . . .' For the first time, McRae seemed to notice Hannah, Helen and Laura's hostile stares. He shuffled his feet and paused to clear his throat.

'But?' Maggie Firth invited him to continue.

'But when I went back with the van this morning to pick him up from where I'd left him, he'd disappeared!'

Hannah, Helen and Laura stood silently by the tall, stained-glass window of the Firths' breakfast-room. Angus Firth had given up trying to understand what was going on in his own house, and taken Bobby out on to the hills. But Maggie Firth and David Moore sat at the table, opposite the scrawny figure of Gordon McRae.

'Maybe we can help, Mr McRae!' Maggie had said brightly, ushering him in. She'd given the girls a secret wink behind the horse-dealer's back.

'It's a case of the missing Shetlands, is it?' David

Moore looked shrewdly from Maggie to McRae.

'A complete mystery,' the man grumbled. Grudgingly he took a cup of tea from the landlady and sipped noisily. 'I didn't give much for the chances of the foal surviving by herself, so I wasn't expecting to see her again. But it stands to reason, a pony like that piebald gelding can't vanish overnight!'

Behind his back, Hannah and Helen shook their heads hard to warn their dad not to say anything.

'You're right,' David agreed. 'But let me get this straight; you were driving south with six ponies. How far had you already driven before you – er – lost two of them?'

'All the way from the Shetland Isles,' McRae said shortly. He sniffed and studied the grubby bandage covering his right hand. 'I bought them from crofters on the island and shipped them over on the ferry. That cost me plenty, let me tell you.'

'So they all belong to you?' the twins' dad double-checked.

'That's what I just said!' the man snapped back. He stood up and turned accusingly towards

Maggie. 'I thought you said you could help.'

'Maybe,' she replied carefully. 'I said maybe we could help.'

'No!' the twins and Laura mouthed from the window. They shook their heads until they almost dropped off.

No way would they give this heartless man the information he needed to recapture Scott and Heather.

But he caught Maggie's eye, then turned suspiciously towards the girls. 'What's going on?'

'N-nothing!' Hannah stammered, feeling her face go bright red.

'Yes, there is!' He advanced a few steps across the room. 'You three know something!'

'N-no!' Helen gulped.

McRae chose to collar Laura, who backed away against the patterned window. 'Come on, spit it out!'

'What?' she quavered.

'Look, I can tell you're hiding something.' He stuck his grubby face close to hers. 'And it doesn't take a genius to know what that something is!'

Laura pressed herself against the window frame, shaking her head.

'You know where my pony is and you're not prepared to tell me!' McRae accused loudly.

Hannah, Helen and Laura held their breaths and said nothing.

'OK, listen!' McRae swung round, pointing an accusing finger at everyone in the room. 'I'm the rightful owner of those animals, and unless you tell me where they are, I walk out of here and go straight to the police!'

Eight

It had begun to rain as Helen, Hannah and Laura led the group of grown-ups to the deserted croft. A soft, warm drizzle covered their hair with shining droplets and dampened their sad faces.

'I'm sorry, girls, but until the RSPCA shows up, there's nothing we can do!' David Moore was as unhappy as they were when McRae had forced the truth out of their friend.

'Laura could have lied!' Helen had felt so bad about Laura telling the horse-dealer where to find Scott and Heather that she'd stormed out of

Glendach House into the garden. Her dad had followed her there.

He'd done his best to comfort her. 'I know this hurts,' he'd said gently. 'And I know how unfair it must seem . . .'

'He's a horrible, cruel man!' Helen hadn't been able to accept that McRae could muscle in and take the ponies back after the way he'd treated them.

'I'll ring the RSPCA again,' her dad had promised, putting an arm round Hannah, who had followed them into the garden.

But to Hannah, it felt as though it was already too late.

'You'll find your ponies in the old barn,' Laura had told McRae quietly, her face white as she pressed back against the breakfast-room window. 'If you stop shouting and calm down, we'll take you there in the car.'

And now this was their last visit to brave little Scott and the frail foal.

They dragged their feet through the wet heather,

as they approached the old croft, knowing that the horse-dealer had parked his van in the very spot where the Moores had broken down the day before. Soon he would be seizing Scott's halter rope and dragging him back down the moor, then bundling Heather into the dark horse-box alongside the five other miserable ponies.

Hannah looked ahead, up the rain-soaked hillside. Behind her, she could hear the low grumble of McRae's voice and the tramp of the grown-ups' feet. And there was Angus Firth, driving the Land Rover across the field to meet then.

'Let's run and say goodbye to the ponies before anyone else gets there,' Hannah suggested to Helen and Laura.

'Do we have to?' Helen kept up reluctantly. Saying goodbye to Scott and Heather was the last thing she wanted to face.

'They'll never understand!' Laura shook her head as she ran. They'd reached the farm gate and begun to cross the overgrown yard. 'The moment they see McRae, they'll think we've let them down!'

'We have!' Helen muttered, following Hannah into the barn.

Scott heard their voices and whinnied a greeting from his stall. They could pick out his sturdy black and white body in the gloom, see the glint of his eyes beneath his shaggy mane. Hannah went over to him and rubbed his neck.

Hearing Heather rustle in the straw, Helen and Laura headed in her direction.

'Look!' Helen gasped as her eyes got used to the dim light.

The foal had decided to stand. She was folding her front legs from the knobbly knee joints, pushing her weight forwards and kneeling. Then she jerked her head and lifted herself. Soon she was up on her feet unaided, giving a pleased little snicker as the girls edged nearer.

'Clever girl!' Laura whispered.

'She's getting stronger!' Helen's eyes filled with tears. It was their feeding and care that had done it.

But they only had a few moments to enjoy the sight. Soon there were shadowy figures at the barn door, and Gordon McRae pushed forward, making straight for Scott's stall.

He'd seized the wooden planks that formed the barricade across the stall, ready to grab Scott's rope and drag him out, when a voice suddenly interrupted.

'I should leave him there if I were you!'

The twins and Laura swung round. It was Angus Firth and he was striding across the barn with Bobby at his heel.

'What's it to do with you?' McRae answered roughly, lifting a plank and throwing it to one side.

Inside the stall, Scott laid his ears back and stamped his feet in warning.

'You might want to listen a moment,' Angus told him calmly. 'I was just clearing up at Brae Croft when there was a phone call . . . for you.'

The horse-dealer paused. 'Who from?'

'From a woman who said she'd be interested in buying a couple of Shetland ponies from you.'

McRae turned round. 'Did she now?'

'Aye. She said she'd heard on the grapevine that you had ponies for sale. I said she'd best come straight on up, otherwise she'd be too late.' Angus delivered the news without expression. He kept a steady eye on McRae as he spoke. 'She's on her way right this minute.'

'Brilliant!' Helen cried. She hugged Scott and made an extra fuss of Heather.

'They're safe!' Hannah breathed. She tilted her head back and gazed up into the dusty roof-beams of the old barn.

'We hope!' Laura added a note of caution. She heard a car wind its way up the hill. Then the engine stopped and a door slammed.

Now there were only minutes to wait before the surprise buyer showed up.

'The woman's here!' McRae shouted from the barn door. 'You girls can bring the ponies out into the yard for her to look at!'

'I'll lead Scott!' Hannah said eagerly. She removed the planks of wood and stepped inside the stall.

'And I'll bring Heather!' Helen stooped to pick straw from the foal's mane and tail.

Laura stood by quietly, taking in every move the ponies made. 'It's still goodbye,' she sighed. 'Last night I dreamed we had them at Doveton Manor. And now . . .'

'I know.' Hannah took Scott's halter-rope and led him slowly across the barn. The pony paused to nudge Laura and nuzzle up to her, as if he too understood.

But there wasn't much time. They could hear McRae outside in the yard, greeting the newcomer in a false, cheery voice. So while Helen tempted Heather out of the barn with a handful of feed, Hannah led Scott smartly on.

'I've got a nice little gelding that I'm sure you'd like!' McRae was telling a woman in a cream sweater and black jodphurs. 'And a six-month-old foal that's just been weaned and is looking for a home.'

Hannah blinked in the daylight. Beside her, Scott came to a standstill. She blinked again, then stared at the woman who had come to buy the ponies.

'It's Jeanie!' Helen cried. She left Heather's side

and hurried across the yard. 'Jeanie – from the riding-school!'

'It's true, I'm looking for Shetlands,' Jeanie told the horse-dealer. She'd greeted the surprised group with a brief, friendly smile, then plunged on into discussing business with McRae.

'They're good-natured little ponies,' the dealer said, the fake smile creasing his face into deep wrinkles. 'And this gelding's a lively one. You wouldn't be disappointed if you took him.'

'Well, let me take a good look at him.' Jeanie moved in and ran expert hands over the pony's legs and flanks. 'I don't like the look of that cut on his cheek,' she pointed out.

'It happened in transit.' McRae sprang back with an explanation. 'The pony must have lost his balance inside the horse-box and pulled on the halter.'

From a distance, Hannah watched anxiously. 'Does Jeanie realise these are the ponies your mum and dad told her about yesterday?' she whispered to Laura.

'She must do.' Laura reminded her that it was Jeanie who had sent the feed and ointment. 'This must be her secret way of trying to rescue Scott and Heather!'

'What a relief!' Helen sighed. She could picture Scott and Heather at Invermore, grazing in the paddock, giving rides to excited children, getting the very best attention from Jeanie and her staff.

'And the foal seems underweight,' Jeanie continued, moving over to examine Heather.

'She lost her mother at four months,' came the prompt excuse. 'I bottle-fed her until she was weaned. And though she's a bit below par, she'll soon make up for lost time when she's settled in with you.'

'Hmm.' Jeanie Watson circled the two ponies who stood patiently in the rainy yard. She glanced at David Moore and Angus and Maggie Firth, as if considering things carefully. 'You say you bought the ponies on Shetland itself? Of course you'd have proof of sale ... documents from the previous owners?'

McRae cleared his throat noisily. 'Normally I

would say yes. But in this case . . .' For the first time he hesitated.

Angus Firth frowned at David Moore. Maggie took a step nearer to Jeanie Watson.

'Whoa, Scott!' Hannah murmured as the pony sensed the suddenly uneasy atmosphere.

'. . . In this case, there's been a bit of a slip-up.' The horse dealer tried to brush the question to one side.

'What kind of a slip-up?' Jeanie wanted to know.

'I had the papers, all official, when I drove on to the ferry at Lerwick. But when I got off at Aberdeen, I found they were missing. I must have left them on the boat by mistake.'

Jeanie shook her head. 'Without the papers, there's no deal,' she told him. 'I can't afford to run the risk.' Once more she glanced at the other adults gathered in the small yard.

'Well, let's not be hasty!' Sensing that he was about to lose a sale, McRae panicked. 'I'm sure the ferry people will find the papers and send them on to me. Then I can post them to you; all legal and above-board.'

'Hmm.' Jeanie still wasn't convinced. She stroked Heather and moved back round to Scott. 'I'd be happier if you could tell me exactly where your bought them.'

'From small crofts here and there,' he blustered. 'Now these two ponies you're looking at came from a village outside Lerwick; Oxhead, I think it was.'

Oxhead. Hannah concentrated and stored the name in her memory.

'I don't think I know it.' Jeanie circled Scott, as if still interested in buying him.

'No, it's just a wee place; a couple of crofts, a pub, a post office.' McRae rambled on, hoping to convince her.

It was enough for Hannah. She sidled up to Helen. 'Help Jeanie to keep him talking,' she whispered.

Helen nodded quickly. 'Where are you going?'

From halfway across the yard, while Jeanie Watson quizzed McRae about Scott and Heather, she mouthed her secret answer. 'To ask Angus if he'll give me a lift to the house. I want to make a phone call. Wait here!'

'Yes, this is the postmaster at Oxhead post office.' A voice crackled down the phone as Hannah stood in the hallway at Glendach House. 'How can I help you?'

Hannah gripped the phone so tight her knuckles turned white. 'I'd like to find out about two Shetland ponies.'

'Ah now!' The man sounded amused. 'Which ponies would that be? We have so many Shetlands on the island.'

'Two piebald geldings. One has a black face with a white star, a black mane and tail, a white patch across his back. And the foal . . .' She paused.

'Ah. Perhaps I know the ponies you mean. And what would you like to know about them?' The postmaster seemed to have plenty of time to answer Hannah's urgent questions.

'Could you tell me the name of their owners?' she gabbled. 'Or rather, the person who last owned them on the island, before he sold them.'

'Sold?' There was pause for thought. 'Now, if it's the ponies I'm thinking of, they haven't been sold.'

'No?' Hannah's heart lurched and skipped a beat. 'Are you sure?'

'Certain.' The voice on the phone was absolutely clear. 'No, those little piebalds are lovely wee horses. There's no way that Jack McLeod would have sold them.'

There was more to come, Hannah felt certain. 'What then?'

'Stolen,' came the reply. 'The ponies disappeared in the dead of night; they were spirited away!'

Nine

Hannah ran like the wind from Glendach House back to the deserted croft. 'Please – please – please let me be on time!' she muttered to herself. She didn't care about the rain, nor the scratches on her legs from the heather and bramble bushes, nor her aching legs and bursting lungs.

'Please don't let Jeanie have said no! Please don't make McRae bundle Scott and Heather into the horrible van!' She hoped with all her heart that her news would get through.

'Wait!' Hannah spied Helen standing at the

roadside. Helen began to run towards her. 'Make them wait!' she cried again.

'Hurry up!' Helen's voice was high-pitched with worry. 'He's forcing Scott into the horse-box! I think he knows that Jeanie's on our side!' She reached Hannah and described what was going on. 'McRae realised that Jeanie wasn't a real customer, and that she was going to accuse him of treating his ponies badly. He got really angry and told us all to clear off out of his way. Now he's dragging Scott up the ramp into the box! He's going to get away with it!'

Hannah forced her legs to keep going. 'Oh no, he's not!' She rounded the bend and saw the tall red van parked at the roadside. She spotted a bunch of grown-ups standing by parked cars. She saw brave little Scott kicking and pulling, heard him whinny and squeal as McRae jerked his halter-rope and tugged him on.

'Make him stop!' Laura cried, breaking away from the group of onlookers and running at the vicious horse-dealer.

McRae shoved her back. 'These are my horses

and I'll deal with them how I want!' he yelled.

'No!' Hannah arrived at the scene and ran up to the dealer. 'They're *not* your horses!'

He turned on her, swinging the dangling rope at her so that it snaked towards her. 'Stay back!' he snarled.

'Scott and Heather are not yours!' she repeated. 'And neither are the ponies in the van.'

'Get lost!' McRae moved as if to shove her out of the way, but David Moore and Angus Firth sprang forward and seized him by the arms.

'Go on, Hannah,' her dad said steadily. He locked the man's arm behind his back and made him double forward in pain.

'You stole them all!' she said, crying with relief and feeling the salt tears mingle with the rain on her cheeks. 'You raided crofts on the Shetland Islands and stole every single one!'

'And here's the photographic evidence of cruelty to the ponies.' David Moore produced the pictures of Scott and Heather that he'd taken the day before. He spread them out on the dashboard of the

inspector's van. The RSPCA man had shown up at last, apologising that it had taken so long to respond to their calls. 'We had an oil-slick emergency to deal with out in Invermore Bay,' he told them. 'It required all our staff to deal with it.'

'See that cut on Scott's cheek!' Hannah pointed out.

'And look how weak and thin Heather was when we found her!' Helen added.

The twins and Laura crowded round the inspector's van. 'Will you punish him?' Laura asked.

The new arrival on the scene nodded. 'I'd like to keep these photographs,' he told them. 'They'll be very useful when we get McRae into court.' He stepped out of the van and glanced in the horse-dealer's direction.

The man stood helplessly by as Jeanie Watson and Maggie Firth unloaded the four ponies tethered inside. His shoulders had slumped, his head hung forward as he watched all the activity in surly silence.

'We're waiting for the police to get here,' the twins' dad explained to the young, fair-haired inspector. 'Before she left Invermore, Jeanie dialled the local station. She tells me she'd been thinking about the problem ever since Geoffrey and Valerie Saunders went to her for help yesterday. This morning she decided it was time to do something about it.

'Everyone knows everyone else in Invermore and up Glendach Pass, so she soon found out that a stranger had rented Brae Croft and she began to put two and two together. That's how she ended up here to help.'

'A team effort.' The inspector summed up the way everyone had played a part in saving the ponies. He smiled at Helen, Hannah and Laura. 'But a special thanks is due to you three.'

They smiled back as yet another car climbed the deserted road. It was a white police car with two uniformed men inside. As Maggie and Jeanie turned the last pony out of the box and led her up the slope and out of sight, the policemen strode towards Gordon McRae.

'What will happen to the ponies now?' Helen asked. Now that the excitement was over and all the horses were saved, she had time to think ahead.

'The police will contact their owners,' the inspector explained as they all strolled away from the road, up the hill, to discover where Maggie and Jeanie had taken the rescued animals. 'And no doubt the owners will arrange to come down and collect them. It shouldn't be long before they're all safely back where they belong.'

Hannah glanced at Laura, but said nothing. *It's a pity*, she thought. *After all this, Laura's dream of having Scott and Heather at Doveton Manor doesn't come true*.

Meanwhile, Helen looked over her shoulder to see the policemen walking to either side of McRae, leading him to the patrol car. The last sight she had of the mean horse-dealer was of him stooping and getting in. The car door slammed and they were off.

'Would you believe it!' David Moore stopped on the brow of the hill.

'What?' Helen and Hannah said. They gazed all round the moor to discover what new thing had surprised him.

'The sun's coming out through the clouds – there's a rainbow!'

And sure enough, an arc of colour lit up the grey sky. It arched over Benn Thurnish and seemed to end on the patch of pasture where the two women had led the ponies.

'Magic!' Hannah murmured.

They gazed at the green grass and the six ponies all contentedly grazing. There was a chestnut, and a white one, a pretty palomino with a pale golden mane and tail, and a funny, stout little black one. Then of course, there was Scott and Heather.

'Another goodbye,' Laura said softly, with regret.

Tomorrow they would move on. As the Moores and Laura drove home, the crofters would travel down from Lerwick to collect their ponies. Meanwhile, Maggie and Jeanie promised to take very good care of each and every one.

'Come on,' Helen said sadly. She led the way to where Scott and Heather stood.

Hannah and Laura followed. No one spoke as

first the foal, and then Scott, recognised the girls and trotted eagerly towards them.

Laura crouched to stroke and rub Heather, tears blurring her eyes. She sniffed and buried her face against the foal's soft black mane. 'You're going to be fine,' she whispered. 'No more horrible horse-boxes, no one to scare you any more!'

Heather whinnied softly and nuzzled up. She pushed her nose against Laura's wet face.

'And you,' Helen told Scott, who stood, legs apart, snickering with pleasure, between her and Hannah. 'You'll be going home.' She too had to wipe the tears from her face.

Hannah sniffed, then hugged the sturdy little pony. He was brave and loyal, friendly and true; the perfect Shetland.

'You might not think so, but this is a happy ending,' she cried. 'Dad has a great story for his magazine, the police and the RSPCA will stop McRae from ever being cruel to horses again, and you're going home with Heather!'

'Then why the tears?' David Moore asked gently, as he joined the girls in the sunny pasture.

'Because . . .' Hannah sobbed, leaning against Scott's neck.

'Because!' Helen echoed. There was happy and happy. This was happy coloured with the sadness of parting. 'Because we don't like goodbyes!'

The sun shone brightly on a green field surrounded by a white fence. The mountains in the background rose steeply towards a blue morning sky. Between the field and the wild, rocky mountains stood a big grey house with a terraced garden, a stable yard, and a long, sweeping drive.

Hannah leaned on the fence and sighed.

'Magic!' Helen murmured.

Two piebald ponies were grazing in the field. One was only half-grown, but lively now and putting on weight. The other was a stocky, strong little horse with a white star on his black forehead.

Scott raised his head and saw the twins. He trotted gladly towards them to say hello . . .

* * *

'Come up quick!' Laura had told them on the phone, her voice bursting with excitement.

'What for?' Helen had asked.

They'd been back from holiday for three days, thinking sadly of Scott and Heather travelling on the ferry to their distant island home.

'Wait and see!' Laura had quickly put down the phone and Helen and Hannah had cycled down to Doveton Manor with a big question mark in their minds.

Their friend had met them at the wide double-gates of the manor house. 'Leave your bikes here and follow me!'

They'd cut across Mr Saunders' smooth lawns, past some tall bushes, round the side of the stables to the white fence surrounding the paddock.

'Close your eyes!' Laura had said at the last minute. 'Wait here!'

Then she'd run back to the stables. The twins had heard hooves clip-clopping over the yard. A gate had swung open and the horses had stepped into the field.

'Now open them!' Standing by the gate, Laura

had waited to see their surprise.

. . . Two piebald ponies grazing in the field. One
was only half-grown . . . The other was a stocky,
strong little horse . . .

'Scott!' Hannah shrieked with delight.

'Heather!' Helen echoed.

They turned to Laura together. 'How come?'

Laura laughed and went to stroke the ponies.
She gave them pieces of apple and watched them
munch.

'It's all thanks to Angus Firth,' she told them.

Helen raised her eyebrows until they disappeared under her fringe.

'I know we all thought he was grumpy,' Laura went on, 'but like Maggie said, his bark was worse than his bite.'

Hannah climbed the fence and jumped down to give Heather a hug. 'Tell us!' she laughed. 'Come on, Laura, what on earth happened?'

Laura took a deep breath. 'Angus decided to ring Jack McLeod, the man who owned Scott and Heather at Oxhead. He explained how we rescued the ponies, and if it hadn't been for us, Heather would probably have died.'

Helen nodded. 'Go on!'

'It turned out Jack McLeod has a daughter called Marie who used to ride Scott. But Marie grew too big for Shetlands, so he's bought her another horse.'

'And what about Heather?' Hannah asked. 'How come the McLeods had just taken on another young Shetland?'

'She belonged to a neighbour at first. But her mother died a few weeks ago, and the McLeods felt sorry for the motherless foal. They said they would adopt her. From the day she arrived at their croft, Scott stepped in and took care of her. Mr McLeod said they were always together – inseparable.'

Hannah nodded and patted Scott gently as Laura went on.

'Well, to cut a long story short, once Mr McLeod heard what we'd done, he . . .' A grin spread across Laura's face as she paused to catch her breath.

'Yes?' Helen pressed. Happiness bubbled up inside as she realised what Laura was going to say.

'He said we should have a reward . . .'

'. . . And?' Hannah stood up and whirled round. Doveton Manor, the mountains, the blue sky started to spin.

Laura laughed with Helen and Hannah. They joined hands in a circle and twirled. Scott raised his head and snickered. Little Heather jumped and kicked for joy.

'He gave the ponies to me!' Laura crowed. She broke hands and spread her arms wide. 'For good! For ever! From now on, this is their home!'

SPOT THE PRISONER
Home Farm Twins 18

Jenny Oldfield

Hannah and Helen's neighbour, Mrs Higham, has a new puppy. But she keeps it shut away behind a high wire fence and, when the twins pass the house, they hear the lonely pup crying. Then, when they go back the next day, they find the puppy running loose. There's no sign of his owner and no reply from the house. Could Mrs Higham have deserted her pup? Or is she in some kind of trouble?

HOME FARM TWINS
Jenny Oldfield

All Hodder Children's books are available at your local bookshop, or can be ordered direct from the publisher. Just tick the titles you would like and complete the details below. Prices and availability are subject to change without prior notice.

Please enclose a cheque or postal order made payable to *Bookpoint Ltd*, and send to: Hodder Children's Books, 39 Milton Park, Abingdon, OXON OX14 4TD, UK. Email Address: orders@bookpoint.co.uk

If you would prefer to pay by credit card, our call centre team would be delighted to take your order by telephone. Our direct line *01235 400414* (lines open 9.00 am–6.00 pm Monday to Saturday, 24 hour message answering service). Alternatively you can send a fax on *01235 400454*.

TITLE		FIRST NAME		SURNAME	

ADDRESS	

DAYTIME TEL:		POST CODE	

If you would prefer to pay by credit card, please complete:
Please debit my Visa/Access/Diner's Card/American Express (delete as applicable) card no:

Signature .... Expiry Date: ....

If you would NOT like to receive further information on our products please tick the box. ❑